Unwrap thi... ...scover a
centipede wh... ...(which
keep getting lost in the wash), a haddock
who falls in love with a mermaid, some
children who find dinosaur tracks in the
playground, a guinea pig who is teaching
himself to read and many other exciting
stories.

Every story tied up in this parcel has been
carefully chosen and tried out by children's
book expert, Pat Thomson. They are all by
top children's authors from around the world,
including Jan Mark, James Marshall and
William Mayne.

Pat Thomson is a well-known author
and anthologist of children's stories. She also
works with teachers as a lecturer and
librarian. She is an Honorary Vice-President
of the Federation of Children's Book Groups.
She is married, has two grown-up children
and lives in Northamptonshire.

Also collected by Pat Thomson
and published by Corgi Books

★ Also available on audio tape.

A Parcel of Stories for 5-Year-Olds

COLLECTED BY
Pat Thomson

Illustrated by
Anthony Lewis

CORGI BOOKS

A PARCEL OF STORIES FOR FIVE YEAR OLDS
A CORGI BOOK : 0 552 54544 9

PRINTING HISTORY
Corgi edition published 1999

3 5 7 9 10 8 6 4 2

Set in 16/20pt Bembo Schoolbook by
Phoenix Typesetting, Ilkley, West Yorkshire.

Corgi Books are published by Random House Children's Books,
61–63 Uxbridge Road, London W5 5SA,
a division of The Random House Group Ltd,
in Australia by Random House Australia (Pty) Ltd,
20 Alfred Street, Milsons Point, Sydney, NSW 2061, Australia,
and in New Zealand by Random House New Zealand Ltd,
18 Poland Road, Glenfield, Auckland 10, New Zealand
and in South Africa by Random House (Pty) Ltd,
Endulini, 5a Jubilee Road, Parktown 2193, South Africa.

Printed and bound in Great Britain by
Cox & Wyman Ltd, Reading, Berkshire.

Acknowledgements

The editor and publisher are grateful for permission to include the following copyright stories:

Jean Chapman, 'Sock Eater', from *Stories to Share*, ed. Jean Chapman (Hodder & Stoughton, 1993). Reprinted by permission of the author.

John Grant, 'Littlenose Meets Two-Eyes', from *The Adventures of Littlenose* (BBC Books, 1972). Reprinted by permission of the author.

Margaret Joy, 'The Dinosaurs' Den', from *Hild at Allotment Lane School* (Faber & Faber, 1987).

Jenny Koralek, 'Marika's Favourite Story', from *A Moon, A Star, A Story* (Blackie). Reprinted by permission of David Higham Associates Limited, © Jenny Koralek 1990.

Jan Mark, 'Haddock' (Simon and Schuster, 1994). Reprinted by permission of Wayland Publishers Limited.

James Marshall, 'Miss Mouse', from *Rats on the Range* (Hamish Hamilton, 1994). Reprinted by permission of Sheldon Fogelman Literary Agency.

William Mayne, 'Barnabas Walks' (Walker Books, 1986). Reprinted by permission of David Higham Associates Limited.

Pamela Oldfield, 'A Shaggy Dog Story' (Blackie, 1990). Reprinted by permission of Serafina Clarke Literary Agency.

Pat Thomson, 'Sody Saleratus' and re-telling of 'The Town Mouse and The Country Mouse', © Pat Thomson, 1998. Reprinted by permission of the author.

Contents

Littlenose Meets Two-Eyes

Littlenose was a boy who lived long, long ago. His people were called the Neanderthal folk. In the days when they lived, the world was very cold. It was called the Ice Age.

There were lots of wild animals. Lions, tigers, bears and wolves had thick furry coats to keep them warm. Even the rhinoceros, and a kind of elephant called a mammoth, were big woolly creatures.

The Neanderthal folk were stocky, sturdy people with short necks and big noses. They were very proud of their noses, which were large and snuffly. Littlenose got his name because his nose was no bigger than a berry.

Littlenose's home was not a house, but a cave where he lived with his father and mother. Near the front of the cave a huge fire was always burning. This kept the family warm, and also frightened away wild creatures, which was just as well because there was no door on the cave.

Sometimes Littlenose was naughty, and that could be dangerous. A child who strayed from his family cave, or loitered on an errand, might be eaten by a sabre-tooth tiger, or squashed flat as a pancake by a woolly rhinoceros.

But today Littlenose had been very naughty indeed. While his parents were hunting, he had let the fire go out.

Now he sat at the back of the cave

and watched Father trying to re-light it. Father had two stones called flints which he banged together to make a spark. (There were no matches in those days.) But he couldn't strike a spark.

'Perhaps you need a new flint,' said Mother.

'I'll need a new son if he lets the fire out again,' grumbled Father. Littlenose expected to be thrown to the bears right away.

However, as they had no fire, Father blocked the cave entrance with rocks to keep out wild beasts. In the morning they had a cold breakfast. Father got ready to go for the flint.

'Have you enough money?' said Mother.

'I think so,' said Father, and pulled out a handful of the coloured pebbles that they used for money.

He kissed Mother goodbye, and was

just going when Littlenose said, 'Can I come too?'

For a moment Father said nothing. Then: 'After the way you behaved, yesterday?' he exclaimed. 'Oh, all right,' and off he went, leaving Littlenose to follow.

'Goodbye, Littlenose,' Mother called after him. 'Be good. And always look both ways before you cross.'

But Littlenose wasn't listening. He was thinking about his secret. He had a pebble of his own. A green pebble, which he had found by the river. He had never been to a market before. But he was sure he would see something worth buying today.

They made their way by a woodland path. Father strode along with his club in his hand, and Littlenose skipped gaily behind him. Ahead, the path was crossed by a broad animal trail. Littlenose was about to dash straight across, when a cuff on the ear nearly knocked him down.

'Don't you *ever* do what Mother tells you?' said Father, angrily. Shamefaced, Littlenose stood on the grass verge and:

Looked right!
Looked left!
And right again!

As he looked right the second time, a herd of woolly rhinoceros came round the bend. He and Father dived into the bushes. They lay hidden as the great beasts lumbered by. Their small eyes blinked through their fur, and their long horns looked very dangerous.

When the rhinos had passed, Littlenose and Father went on their way.

Littlenose felt he had been walking for ever. But soon they left the woods and began climbing a grassy hillside. At last they came to a circle of trees. Littlenose realized that this was the market.

There seemed to be hundreds of people. Littlenose hadn't thought there were so many people in the whole world. He trotted behind Father, and he was bumped, pushed, trodden on, tripped over and shouted at. The sheer noise made him speechless – but not for long.

Suddenly: 'I'm hungry,' he said.

'You're always hungry,' grumbled Father. But he bought each of them a steaming hot hunk of meat from a man who was roasting a deer over a fire.

Then he went over to an old man who was sitting under a tree. There was a sign with his name on it.

At least, Littlenose thought it was his name. When he got closer, he saw that it had once read:

But the words were faded with the
weather. Only 'Skin' and 'Flint' could
be made out now. Most people thought
it was the old man's name.

Neither Father nor the old man
seemed in a hurry to settle about the
new flint. Littlenose soon grew bored.

He wandered through the market,
looking here and listening there.
Everyone was bustling about buying
the things they couldn't find or make
for themselves. There were bone and
ivory combs, and needles and pins.
There were strange nuts, fruits and
berries. And there were furs. Hundreds
and hundreds of furs. From tiny mink
and ermine to enormous white
bearskins from the far north.

But Littlenose didn't see anything he

wanted to buy. He had almost decided
to keep his pebble for another day,
when, over the heads of the crowd, he
saw a sign.

Littlenose pushed forward. In a clear
space, a little man stood on a tree stump.

'Five red pebbles I'm bid,' he
shouted. 'Five! Going at five! Going!
Going! GONE! Sold to the gentleman
in the lion skin for five red pebbles.'

The gentleman in the lion skin
counted out his money. Then a huge
woolly mammoth was led over to him.

'Oh,' thought Littlenose, 'if only I
could buy one of those. I would march
home, leading him by his trunk.
Everyone would cheer. When I got
home I would . . . oh, dear no! I forgot.
I'm not even allowed pet mice in the

cave. Anyway, a mammoth would hardly get its tail through the door. And that's about all I could buy with my pebble.'

And, feeling very sad, Littlenose walked away. He sat down by the mammoth pen to rest. The pen was built of huge logs and was too high to see over.

Suddenly he jumped. Something soft and warm had tickled his neck.

It was a trunk – a very little one.

Littlenose looked through the bars of the pen. He saw the smallest, woolliest, saddest mammoth you could imagine. He climbed up and reached over the top rail to stroke its furry ears.

Suddenly he was seized by the scruff of his neck. A voice said: 'And what are you doing, young man?'

It was the man who owned the mammoths.

'Please,' said Littlenose, 'I was just looking at the mammoth.'

'Don't tell stories,' said the man. 'We've sold them all.'

But at that moment the trunk came through the bars again. It tickled the man's leg and he dropped Littlenose.

'They've done it again,' the man shouted to his assistant, who came running. 'Slipped in a reject! It's much too small to sell. And look, the eyes don't match! One's red and one's green. Who's going to buy this sort of animal?'

'I will,' said Littlenose, holding out his pebble.

Looking very relieved the man said, 'Well, I can't charge you more than eight white pebbles for a reject.' He took the green pebble from Littlenose, and gave him two white ones as change. The assistant opened the pen, and the little mammoth trotted out.

'One red eye and one green eye,' said Littlenose. 'That makes two eyes. I shall call you that. Come along, Two-Eyes.'

Littlenose stopped and bought a bundle of bone needles for Mother with his last two pebbles. The market was almost deserted now.

He started looking for Father, but Father found him first.

'Where *have* you been?' he shouted.

'Do you like my mammoth?' asked Littlenose.

'Mammoth? MAMMOTH?' roared Father. 'Are you playing with other people's property? Take it back where you found it. No, wait, we haven't time.' He waved his arms in the air, and gave a loud yell. Two-Eyes went scampering away into the trees.

'But he's mine. I *bought* him,' wailed Littlenose.

But Father wasn't listening – he was

already striding away down the hillside. Littlenose hurried after him. The evening mist began to close in, and the sun became a dull red ball low in the sky.

'Don't dawdle, you'll get lost,' called out Father. But Littlenose kept tripping in the long grass. Each time he looked up it was darker, and even harder to see his father.

He ran on, stumbling and tripping. Then he fell!

When he got up again, he was alone. 'Father!' he called. 'FATHER!' But all he heard was the echo of his own voice.

He began to run. He had never been lost before, and he was very frightened. All sorts of terrible things might be waiting in the mist to jump out at him. As he ran, the sun set. It became pitch dark . . .

All around him he could hear animals growling and snorting. They rustled in the undergrowth, and brushed past him as he ran. He stopped to catch his breath. There was a sound behind him. It was growing louder.

Littlenose began to run again. But, as fast as he ran, the noise came closer. Suddenly he tripped again and fell.

Too frightened to move, Littlenose lay with his eyes closed. The sound grew louder. He could hear an animal breathing, but he dared not look up.

At the cave, Mother looked out as darkness fell. There was a sound of footsteps, and Father groped his way in.

'Where's Littlenose?' asked Mother.

'Isn't he here?' said Father. 'I thought the young rascal must have hurried home ahead of me.'

'Oh,' said Mother, 'he must be lost out there in the dark. You must find him!'

Quickly, Father lit the fire, took a

branch for a torch, and turned back the way he had come.

The mist had gone and the moon was shining. The path lay clear before him. There were animal sounds among the trees. But there was no sign of Littlenose.

Then something moved towards him. Father's torch glinted on a pair of eyes. One red eye. One green eye. It was a small mammoth, and sitting on its back was Littlenose.

'Hello, Father,' he said. 'I got lost, and Two-Eyes followed me and brought me home.'

Mother saw the strange procession approaching the cave. Father was leading Two-Eyes by the trunk. Littlenose, his head nodding, sat on the mammoth's back.

A few moments later, Mother was tucking Littlenose in bed. He held out a little bundle. 'I bought you some needles at the market,' he said, and fell asleep.

The little mammoth was patiently waiting outside. Father took its trunk gently in his hand. He led it past the fire and into the corner where Littlenose slept. With a contented sigh and looking for all the world like an enormous ball of wool, Two-Eyes fell asleep as well.

This story is by John Grant.

Miss Mouse

When Thomas J. Cat looked out of his
window and saw who was standing
on his front doorstep, he couldn't believe
his tired old eyes. It was a mouse. She
was wearing a hat covered with daisies,
in one hand she carried a small leather
purse, and in the other a wicker suitcase
tied up with string. Her skirt was a
coarse wool, as it was the dead of winter.

'Dinner time!' exclaimed Thomas to
himself. 'She's awfully small, but
perhaps I can stretch it out with
chopped carrots and celery.'

The doorbell rang insistently.

'Yoo-hoo!' called out the mouse.

Thomas J. Cat threw on his bathrobe and opened the door a crack. If she sees I'm a tomcat, she'll scamper away, he thought. And I am much too old and sickly for a chase.

'Who is it?' he called out.

'My name is Miss Mouse,' said the mouse. 'I've come in response to your advertisement for a housekeeper. I have references.'

She began to fumble about in her purse.

The tomcat hadn't the slightest idea what the mouse was talking about.

'This *is* 93 Hollow Road, is it not?' said Miss Mouse.

The tomcat was about to inform her that it was 89 Hollow Road, when he thought better of it.

'Er, yes indeed, 93, that's me,' he said.

'May I come in?' said Miss Mouse. 'It's chilly out here.'

'By all means,' said the tomcat, throwing open the door, but remaining behind it.

Miss Mouse stepped over the threshold.

'Why are you standing behind the door?' she said.

'Er,' said the tomcat. 'I'm ashamed of my appearance.'

'I see,' said Miss Mouse.

Then she looked about the tomcat's messy living room.

'My, my,' she said. 'I'll have to start in right away. That is, if I have the job. You won't regret it, I do good work.'

The tomcat thought for a minute. Certainly he could use some straightening up around the house. In the past few years he'd really let things slide. And when all the work was

finished, *then* he could eat the mouse —
around snack time. And he wouldn't
even have to pay her a penny.

'Excellent,' said the tomcat. 'The job
is yours.'

Miss Mouse inspected the pantry and
the area under the sink.

'You have no detergents or cleansers!'
she said. 'I'll just pop around the corner
to the market and buy some things. I'll
need about twenty dollars.'

The tomcat found a twenty-dollar bill
in his robe pocket.

I was planning to spend this at the
races, he thought.

Miss Mouse took the twenty.

'I'll be back in a jiffy. Perhaps you
can make us a nice pot of tea?'

'By all means,' said the tomcat,
who'd never made tea in his life.

'And by the way,' said Miss Mouse, 'I
know you're a tomcat, so you can

come out from behind that door.'

'How could you tell?' said the tomcat.

'One knows these things,' said Miss Mouse. 'But I'm sure we'll get along just fine.'

Miss Mouse firmly believed that kindness, industry, and generosity of spirit could tame the most ferocious of creatures.

She went out the front door.

'Perhaps I've made a mistake,' said the tomcat. 'What if she doesn't come back? Ah well, you just have to trust.'

He went into the kitchen to try and rustle up some tea.

When Miss Mouse returned, carrying two shopping bags full of detergents and cleansers, she heard a pitiful groaning coming from the kitchen. The tomcat had badly burned his paws while making tea. He was rolling about the floor in considerable pain.

'Dear, oh dear,' said Miss Mouse. 'We'll have to attend to this immediately. Fortunately I have a first aid kit in my suitcase.'

'Hurry,' said the tomcat. 'I'm dying!'

Miss Mouse retrieved her first aid kit, applied some soothing ointment to the burned paws, and wrapped them with bandages.

'Snug,' she said. 'And now you must get into bed and do absolutely nothing. We don't want these paws to become infected. Let me help you to your room.'

The tomcat leaned on Miss Mouse, and together they haltingly made their way to the bedroom.

'Holy cow!' cried Miss Mouse. 'This is worse than the living room. It will take me *days* to clean.'

'I'm somewhat disorganized,' said the tomcat, slipping in between the grey sheets.

For the rest of the morning and most of the afternoon, Miss Mouse worked in the living room.

'Tut, tut, tut,' she said. 'And cats have the reputation of being so clean and orderly.'

She swept out a large ball of fur that had accumulated under the sofa.

At four o'clock the tomcat, who had been dozing and dreaming of all *sorts* of tasty things, was awakened by a gentle tap at his bedroom door.

'Come in,' he said.

Miss Mouse came in struggling with a large tea tray piled high with sardine sandwiches and potato chips. There was even a mug of hot cocoa. She sat on the side of the bed and popped the sandwiches into the tomcat's open mouth. 'Yum, yum,' said the tomcat.

When snack time was over, the tomcat felt all plump and rosy.

'I think I'll go back to sleep now,' he said.

'Oh no,' said Miss Mouse. 'I have to change these filthy bedclothes.'

And she put the tomcat, all bundled up, on the back porch while she cleaned and tidied up the bedroom.

She was in the bedroom quite some time and the tomcat grew concerned and went to investigate.

The bedroom smelled of cleanser and room freshener and was as neat as a pin. Miss Mouse was sitting propped up on the bed and absorbed in a thick book.

'I found that on the top shelf in the closet,' said Miss Mouse.

'It must have been left by the previous tenant,' said the tomcat. 'I don't read much myself.'

'Well, it's wonderful,' said Miss Mouse. 'Just listen to this . . .'

The tomcat sat beside the bed, and

Miss Mouse began to read.

It was a story about a treasure ship with billowing sails, a swashbuckling hero, and wicked pirates. An hour later Miss Mouse finished reading.

'And the evil pirate Captain Blackheart was never seen again. The End.'

The tomcat, whose pulse was racing, was enchanted.

'More!' he cried.

'We'll read another tomorrow,' said Miss Mouse. 'I must cook dinner. We're having a tuna casserole.'

Days went by and Miss Mouse and the tomcat established a fixed and pleasant routine.

While the tomcat slept late, Miss Mouse tidied up the house, went shopping, and cooked. Every day just after snacks she read a story from the thick book. It was the tomcat's favourite hour. Miss Mouse read thrilling stories about dinosaurs, cowboys, and space explorers. And the tomcat could never get enough.

'Things are working out quite nicely, aren't they?' said Miss Mouse. 'I hope you are pleased with my work.'

'Indeed,' said the tomcat.

But one day Miss Mouse discovered something that shook her to the core of her being. While straightening up once again the tomcat's cluttered bedroom, she spotted a newspaper that was open to the home section. It was a full page of recipes of various mouse dishes. Several of the recipes were circled in ink. Miss Mouse had to sit down and catch her breath.

'Really!' she said. 'I see my philosophy of kindness and generosity of spirit has not paid off. A cat is still a cat.'

She checked the newspaper again, just to be certain she hadn't overlooked something. Perhaps the tomcat was planning to substitute parsnips or potatoes for the mouse meat in the recipe. But no such luck. There in the tomcat's own shaky handwriting was a shocking notation beside this recipe:

MOUSE MOUSSE

Boil a large mouse, as large as you can catch.

Brown an onion.

Place in a blender, turn on to finely chopped, for five minutes.

Scoop out the mixture and place in a buttered pie tin.

Place in the refrigerator overnight. Serves one.

'Yum, yum,' the tomcat had written.

'I'll have this one for my Easter dinner.'

Miss Mouse consulted her calendar. Easter was several weeks away. If she used her wits, she would be able to stay in the snug tidy house a bit longer. On the day before Easter she would – sadly – leave.

The tomcat entered the room and Miss Mouse hurriedly hid the newspaper behind her.

'Shall we read another story?' she said.

'Excellent,' said the tomcat. And he settled himself on the bed.

Miss Mouse opened the thick book, but she was disappointed to find that all the remaining stories were about love and romance – entirely unsuitable to read to a tomcat who loved adventure.

He'll soon grow tired of them, and then there's no telling what he'll do, she thought.

'I'm waiting,' said the tomcat.

Miss Mouse cleared her throat and pretended to read. 'Once upon a time in a dark and smelly cave, there lived an evil dragon.'

'Oh goody,' said the tomcat. 'This is going to be a hot one.'

Miss Mouse continued to make up her story, all the while pretending to read from the book. It was all about a brave knight and how he defeated the evil dragon.

'This is the best of all,' said the tomcat.

Weeks passed. Sometimes Miss Mouse told stories that were scary. The tomcat's fur stood on end. Sometimes the tales were creepy.

'Ooh,' said the tomcat.

And every day Miss Mouse checked off the calendar.

On the day before Easter, while the

tomcat was dozing, Miss Mouse packed up her wicker suitcase, wrote a hurried note, and tiptoed out of the house. At the corner of Cedar and Maple she caught a streetcar for the train station.

When the tomcat awoke, he was miffed at not finding Miss Mouse who always brought in his tea and then 'read' him a story. But Miss Mouse was nowhere about. Pinned to the back of the sofa was the following note (in Miss M's neat little handwriting):

Dear Thomas

I know what you are planning to have for your Easter dinner. That is too much of a sacrifice for me to make. So I must save myself. I am leaving.

Yours truly.
Miss Mouse

P.S. There is a casserole in the refrigerator

'Rats!' cried the tomcat. 'She has left me! I wasn't *really* going to eat her!'

But in his heart of hearts he knew the opposite was true.

On the local train to Trenton Miss Mouse gazed out the rain-streaked window. She would pay a visit to her Aunt Tillie before looking for further employment.

'No cats this time,' she said out loud, startling the passenger in the next seat.

In the following days the tomcat grew weaker and weaker. He'd become used to being waited on, and TV frozen dinners were no longer to his taste. And more to the point, he missed Miss Mouse's stories. (He even may have missed Miss Mouse herself, hard to say.) A day without one of Miss Mouse's stories was a day without sunshine. He tried to make up his own stories, but found it was not so easy to do. 'Once upon a time . . .' was as far as he could get. He knew of course that Miss Mouse had been making up her stories for quite some time now. 'She always held the book upside down,' he said fondly.

To keep the stories in his memory the tomcat wrote them out in a notebook. As his paws were still weak and shaky, it took him several more days. Copying out the stories made him sad, and finally he fell into a swoon.

The doorbell rang, and the tomcat flew to open it. It was Miss Mouse.

'Had enough?' she said.

The tomcat was overjoyed to see her.

'Please come back,' he said.

'Things will have to improve,' said Miss Mouse. 'You must give up eating mouse meat,' she said. 'And I want it in writing.' And she thrust a legal document under his nose for him to sign.

'Anything,' said the tomcat.

'Now let's have a nice hot dinner,' said Miss Mouse, stepping into the kitchen.

'And then can we have a story?' asked the tomcat.

'Of course,' said Miss Mouse.

And that is the end of the story of Miss Mouse and the tomcat. Except that perhaps you'd care to know that the tomcat sent off Miss Mouse's stories to one of the better publishers, who snapped them right up. And with the arrival of Miss Mouse's money from the publisher, they were able to live a far more comfortable life. They were even able to hire full-time help.

This story is by James Marshall.

The Dinosaurs' Den

Mrs Hubb, the school secretary, came hurrying along the corridor towards Class 1. She put her hand on the classroom door handle, then stopped. There was a large notice stuck on the door. She read it aloud:

'Take a deep breath and count up to ten,
Then come on in to the Dinosaurs' Den.'

'My goodness me,' thought Mrs

Hubb. 'That sounds a bit dangerous. But I'll have to go in, Miss Mee is waiting for this sticky tape.'

She went into the classroom and gasped. Hanging from the ceiling were branches and leaves. Stretching all the way along the opposite wall was a long pool of water with plants growing in it and tufts of rushes along its edges. Standing in the water was an enormously long dinosaur. His back and neck touched the ceiling, and he was chewing a mouthful of pondweed.

'He's our diplodocus,' said Barbara.

'And look up in the branches,' said Hild. 'There's some pterodactyls, ready to take off.'

'And look out – on the wall behind you!' said Pete.

Mrs Hubb swung round and gasped again. Coming out from between the tree trunks was a giant creature. It was

walking upright, holding its front paws out, ready to grab something to eat. Its jaws were open, and it was baring its pointed teeth.

'That's a tyrannosaurus rex,' said Wendy. 'I made his claws with foil.'

'Look over here,' said Mary. 'This is a triceratops. I folded the paper to make the frills on his neck – don't you think they're good?'

'And have you seen our fossils?' asked Ian, pulling Mrs Hubb over to the window-sill. 'Do you see this one? It's coprolite – that's dinosaur dung, turned to stone – honest it is.'

There was so much to see, Mrs Hubb didn't know where to look next.

'My goodness,' she said. 'What a wonderful dinosaurs' den you've made. It's a pity you haven't a real dinosaur; it would feel quite at home in here.'

She gave Miss Mee the sticky tape

and went out to ring the hometime bell.

'Now do up your zips and buttons,' said Miss Mee. 'It's bitterly cold outside: it's cold enough for snow.'

Snow did fall in the night; not very deep – just enough to spread a beautiful white cover over roofs, gardens and roads. When Hild woke up, the bedroom was full of brightness. She sat up and peeped round the curtain.

'Snow!' she cried. 'There's snow everywhere – look, Trudi – wake up and look!'

'I've seen snow before,' grunted Trudi, pulling the quilt over her face. She wasn't a bit interested. But Hild was really excited. She loved snow. She loved the beautiful look of it and the cold smell of it; she loved letting snowflakes melt on her tongue or dabbling her fingers in its softness.

She dressed quickly and ran

downstairs; she didn't want to waste a single moment. She pulled on her coat and unbolted the back door. The garden lay smooth and white, like the top of an iced cake. She stepped slowly across the snow. Then she turned and looked behind her; footprints led from the door to where she stood. She bent over to look at the snow more carefully. Now she could see other footprints, tiny ones, tracks of birds or other little creatures which had been in the garden earlier in the morning. Hild turned round and walked slowly back to the door.

Now she could see another set of tracks, large footprints, which led down the side of the house to the bottles of milk on the doorstep; that must have been the milkman in his wellington boots. Hild wondered what other sorts of footprints there were: she'd like to see what sort of tracks a tiger would make in the snow – or a giraffe – or a kangaroo – or even one of the dinosaurs they'd been talking about at school. She suddenly had an amazing idea.

'Great!' she said giggling to herself. 'I'll play a trick; they'll never guess.'

A few minutes later, after a quick breakfast of a banana and a bag of crisps, she banged the door shut and was on her way up Allotment Lane. She was so early that the footprints she made were the first to mark the fresh snow. She laughed to herself as she pressed her feet down slowly and carefully along the middle of the lane. Soon she turned in through the school gate and stepped across the white playground. She hung her coat up on its peg. Then she put something secret that made her laugh into a carrier bag, and hung that up on her peg too.

Everything was strange and quiet – she

realized that she was the first person in school. She tiptoed into Class 1 and sat in the book corner, looking at a book. Then she heard Miss Mee come in and went to talk to her.

'Hello, Hild,' said Miss Mee. 'You beat me to it today.'

'I've been playing a trick,' grinned Hild.

'What sort of a trick?' asked Miss Mee. 'Nice or nasty?'

'Oh, just funny,' said Hild. 'You know our Trudi, don't you?'

'Yes, of course I do,' said Miss Mee, rather surprised at the question.

'Did you know she went snorking last summer?' asked Hild.

'Snorking?' said Miss Mee in a puzzled voice. 'Do you mean snorting, like pigs do?'

'No, snorking,' said Hild. 'Under the water, with flippers and a sort of tube in her mouth to breathe through, and goggles . . .'

'Oh, *snorkelling*, Hild – you mean snorkelling. Is that what your Trudi did?'

'Yes, snorkelling, that's right,' said Hild. 'Well, I've brought a carrier bag with things in to show you. It's hanging on my peg, it's—'

She didn't finish what she was saying, because the twins burst into the classroom.

'Miss Mee, Miss Mee, we came up the lane, and there's monster tracks, right up the middle of the lane.'

Then Paul and Michael came hurrying in.

'Hey, Miss Mee, we've just come up the lane – we followed some giant footprints and they came across the playground right into school!'

Nasreen and Mary came in next.

'Guess what – there's dinosaur

footprints all the way up the lane!'

Soon lots of people were trying to tell Miss Mee about the dinosaur tracks in the snow. Miss Mee wanted to see them for herself, so the children crowded round her and led her outside — all except Hild. There in the playground, leading from the lane, were huge flat footprints, bigger than those made by any person. They led straight into school.

'Do you think they're brontosaurus footprints?' asked Imdad.

They all stared at the tracks.

'No, they'd be bigger,' said Ian. 'A brontosaurus was as big as fifteen elephants.'

'Perhaps it's a pterodactyl,' said little Larry.

'No, silly, that used to fly — it wouldn't *walk* up the lane, would it?'

'It might be a stegosaurus,' suggested Stevie.

'Or a triceratops,' said Mary.

They stared again at the huge footprints. They were all wondering the same thing.

'Do you think it's a tyrannosaurus rex?' whispered Brenda.

Everyone looked round nervously, hoping a tyrannosaurus rex wouldn't come lumbering out, looking for fresh meat. Michael said slowly, 'If the footprints go into school and don't come out again, that means he's still in school somewhere.'

They all gasped. A dinosaur wandering round Allotment Lane School! Barbara shivered.

'Let's go back in again, quick,' she said.

They swarmed back into the warm classroom, and shut the door firmly. Hild was there on her own, making a plasticine diplodocus.

'You should have seen the footprints, Hild,' said Pete excitedly. He moved his hands to show her how huge the footprints were. 'They were long and fat with sort of toe shapes.'

'That wouldn't be toes,' said Hild. 'That'd be claws, sharp claws . . .'

'Did you see a dinosaur go past while we were outside?' asked Larry.

'Well, I might have heard a sort of roaring noise,' nodded Hild.

Everyone gasped and looked at her.

'And a sort of loud hissing . . .' she went on. 'And a dreadful sort of grunting, like some monster was getting hungry and looking for food . . .'

'Oh!' shrieked everyone, eyes wide with fright. 'Where? Where's it gone? Where is it?'

'Just over there by the coat hooks,' said Hild calmly. 'Shall I show you? I'm not scared.'

Everyone pressed close to Miss Mee. Little Larry clutched her skirt. Holding their breath, they watched Hild go to her coat hook. She lifted down her carrier bag and turned to look at them all. There was a long silence.

'Where's the dinosaur, then?' whispered Nasreen.

'In this bag,' said Hild.

There was another long silence, while they all stared at her.

'It's the things our Trudi had for snorking,' she explained.

'Snorkelling,' said Miss Mee.

'Yes, that's right,' said Hild.

She opened the bag and took out a snorkel, some goggles – and a huge pair of rubber flippers. She fitted them over her feet to show everyone.

'I wore them up the lane,' she giggled. 'I wanted to see what sort of tracks they'd make. It was a track trick.'

Her fat little cheeks grew bright pink and she giggled again.

'The dinosaur was me,' she said.

Everyone stared at her for several moments. Then suddenly, Paul began to laugh, then Michael, then Asif spluttered with laughter, and the twins and Laura started to giggle too. Soon everybody was laughing at Hild's trick; even Miss Mee's shoulders were shaking.

'Ooh, you rotten meanie, Hild Hooson!' exclaimed Brenda, still giggling. 'You had us all dead scared.'

'But it was a good trick,' said Hild. 'Wasn't it? And I bet they're the best dinosaur tracks you've ever seen — aren't they? Aren't they?'

And everyone had to nod and laugh and say that they were.

This story is by Margaret Joy.

Barnabas Walks

Barnabas walks when all the scholars
have left the schoolroom and gone hip-
hooraying home.

When the blackboard chalk-dust
floats in the setting sun and the desks
are still; when the ink is silent and the
clock asleep; then Barnabas comes out
of his house on a shelf.

Scholars call it a hutch, but to
Barnabas it is a house, with a front
door, a dining room with hay, a
bedroom with straw.

Barnabas opens the front door.

Not every guinea pig can open his front door. But not every guinea pig is learning to read.

The scholars can do it, thinks Barnabas. And they are not here all day or every day. They never come on church bell day or football day outside.

Perhaps they come in holiday time when I'm not here, all except Willow and Robin.

Barnabas spends holidays next door at Willow's house. Willow and Robin are sisters that look after him in holiday time.

Nimrod from across the square comes to see him there, without Moss, his dog.

Tonight Barnabas opens his front door.

No-one knows he can do it. He does. It creaks, ghostly, ghostly, in the quiet schoolroom.

Barnabas comes out.

He goes to look for his reading book.

He climbs down from the shelf to the back of a chair.

He climbs to a desk top. 'Hello,' he says to inkwell, and wishes. The ink looks black.

He climbs to the seat of a chair and down a box to the floor. He goes to the middle of the room.

A hungry scholar has left a crumb, a chip, a pea as big as a marble that bounced away from dinner.

Barnabas eats them all carefully. He does not want chewing gum again. It lasted a whole week once, then Willow and Nimrod had to trim his fur with school scissors. He liked being picked up and stroked and rubbing noses, but not the snip scissors.

He finds his book in a corner no-one tidies.

The first page is A, the next page is B, after that is C.

Barnabas has looked at the end to see what happens.

Z happens. He does not know how they can be so clever. Now he will read the middle.

He is so busy he does not hear the schoolroom door open.

He does not hear two scholars come in for something.

He does not hear them go out with the thing they wanted.

Barnabas reads all the way to E. He is then hungry.

He walks across the floor. He finds a crisp. He is still hungry. What is one crisp among so many teeth?

He goes home. Up the box, on the seat of the chair, on the desk, on the back of the chair.

Careful about this part, thinks Barnabas, getting up from the floor and starting again.

Lucky not to break a whisker, he thinks, going up the second time.

On the shelf again he opens his front door.

He *tries* to open his front door.

He is where it should be.

How hard it is to do, and all that good food inside.

There is no front door.

There is no house. It has gone.

While he read to E, scholars came and took his house.

They thought it was a hutch. They thought he was in it. They were being kind because it is holiday now.

But Barnabas was reading D and E, an exciting bit.

Perhaps it was too exciting. I should go back and read C again, he thinks. Last time I read it my house was here when I got back.

He looks round the shelf first. No

house is there at all. He sits down where his bed should be.

No straw. Only the bare, cold, shelf.

In the dining room no hay, no dish of food.

He climbs down, down, down, to the floor.

He finds a stick of straw. He finds a wisp of hay. One is in the middle of the room, one is near the door.

He finds a leaf he knows. He was saving it for supper. It is just outside the schoolroom door. He tidies it up.

He finds another straw. He knows it. A guinea pig knows his own bed.

Now he is in the school yard. No scholars play here tonight.

There is some friendly hay. He sits on it and eats it.

Something comes on to the yard wall and sees him. It licks its lips and stands there very still. A tail twitches from side to side. Two eyes watch.

Barnabas does not like the twitching and the watching. He finds a trail of oats and seeds and follows that.

The thing on the wall crouches. It is a hunting, hungry cat from a ratty farmyard.

Barnabas eats one oat. The cat thinks of eating Barnabas.

The cat thinks it had better get on with it, because there are noises nearby.

Willow in the garden shed at home finds Barnabas is not in bed. Oh, oh.

Robin at the landing window sees him in the school yard. Oh, oh, oh.

Nimrod, the other side of the road, lets Moss his dog go for a walk. She has been in all day, curled up with her puppies. She needs a run, and her supper.

Robin falls downstairs. Willow trips over her.

The cat is at the edge of the wall.

Now I shall never know what happens between E and Z, thinks Barnabas. I shall only know what happens ever after Z.

The cat is in the air, eyes cruel.

Moss comes into the school yard.

I think HELP comes after E, says Barnabas. He says it once or twice.

He goes on eating. A well-brought-up guinea pig goes on eating.

Moss runs at the cat. The cat goes away fast, as if it just learned flying.

Dear me, says Moss, and licks Barnabas and picks him up.

'HELP,' says Barnabas again. If it's not one thing it's another. Moss's lick is very sticky.

Supper time, says Moss. She takes him home, and puts him among the puppies, who are all his size and shape and colour.

They are A, B, C, D, and me is E, thinks Barnabas.

Willow and Robin run in and find him.

'They all squeak the same,' says Nimrod, and gives him back. 'YELP,' say puppies, 'HELP,' says Barnabas.

He goes back to his house. Willow and Robin dry him dry of lick while he eats a splendid carrot.

Next term, says Barnabas, all the way from E to Z. And perhaps one day the numbers too. But I'm glad Moss can't count.

This story is by William Mayne.

Sody Saleratus
(A joining-in story.
Say *so-dee-sal-er-aah-tus*.)

Did you ever meet a bear in the forest?
Once, there was a time when there
were no great cities and highways in
America, just forests and narrow paths
and in the forests, there were bears.

People lived in houses built from logs
and did their own baking. And one thing
they loved to eat were delicious, crumbly
scones. Now, if you want scones to be
delicious, to be light and fluffy and rise in
the oven, then you must use baking

powder. In those days, at that time, people called it 'sody saleratus'.

One morning, Ma was all ready to bake when she looked in the cupboard and there was no sody saleratus.

'Oh my!' she said. 'I can't bake scones without sody saleratus. That boy Billy will have to get along to the store and fetch me some.'

And she called, 'Billy, Billy, come right here.'

'What do you want, Ma?'

'Go to the store and fetch me some sody saleratus. Hurry back and don't play in the forest.'

So Billy set off along the forest path to walk to the little town where the store sold everything. As he crossed the wooden bridge, he shouted, 'Sody, sody, saleratus!' Then he walked into town and went across to the store.

'Are you running messages for your

ma, Billy?' smiled the storekeeper who knew him well.

'Ma's run right out of sody saleratus,' he answered.

So the storekeeper sold him a box of sody saleratus and he set off for home straight away.

He had just got as far as the bridge when, from behind a tree, out stepped a big brown bear.

'Dinner time!' growled the bear and he swallowed Billy whole *and* the box of sody saleratus!

At home, Ma waited. 'He must be in town by now,' she said. She waited some more. 'He must be on his way back,' she said. She waited even longer. 'That boy! He must be playing in the forest! And here's me waiting and needing that sody saleratus!' She called, 'Milly, Milly, come right here.'

'What do you want, Ma?'

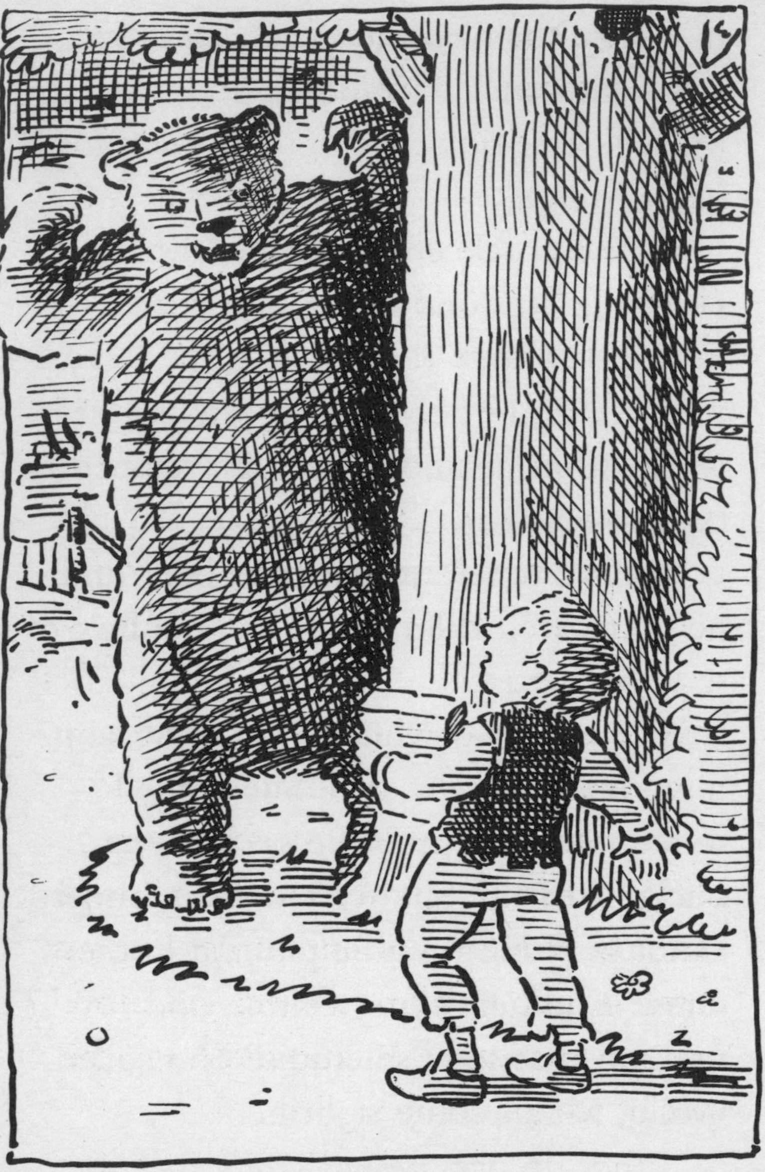

'Go to the store and fetch me some sody saleratus. Hurry back and don't play in the forest.'

So Milly set off along the forest path and as she crossed the bridge, she chanted, 'Sody, sody, sody saleratus.'

She didn't see the bear but the bear saw her.

'What brings you into town, Milly?' smiled the shopkeeper. 'I just sold your brother a box of sody saleratus.'

'He hasn't come back,' said Milly.

'I guess he's playing in the forest. Best take another box if your ma's waiting.'

So Milly set off for home straight away. She had just got as far as the bridge when the big brown bear stepped out and growled, 'Dinner time! I've just eaten a little boy and I'll eat you, too,' and he swallowed Milly whole *and* the box of sody saleratus.

Ma waited. 'She must be in town by now,' she thought. She waited some more. 'She must be on her way back by now.' She waited even longer. 'Those children! They've both stopped to play in the forest. And here's me waiting and needing that sody saleratus!'

She called Grandpa.

'Grandpa, Grandpa, come right here.'

'What do you want, my dear?'

'Those children aren't back and I can't get my baking done. Will you hurry down to the store and bring me some sody saleratus? And if you see those naughty children, just lead them home by their ears!'

Grandpa set off along the path and as he crossed the bridge, he grumbled, 'Sody, sody, sody saleratus.'

He didn't see the bear but the bear saw him.

Grandpa walked straight into

the store. 'Have you seen Billy and Milly today?' he asked.

'I certainly have,' answered the storekeeper. 'I sold them both a box of sody saleratus.'

'Then they must both be playing in the forest. They'll catch it when I catch them. But just in case I don't find them, please give me another box of sody saleratus. Their ma's waiting for it.'

Grandpa set off for home straight away. He had just got as far as the bridge when the big brown bear stepped out and growled, 'Dinner time! I've just eaten a little boy and a little girl and I'll eat you, too.' And he swallowed Grandpa whole *and* the box of sody saleratus.

Now, that bear had eaten more than he usually did and he lay down in the sun, in a clearing in the forest, and soon began to snore.

Ronf, ronf. And the sun shone.

Ronf, ronf. And the day grew warmer.

Ronf, ronf. And something inside the bear began to rise and swell. It was the three boxes of sody saleratus!

Soon, the bear looked like a balloon. Still the sun shone and the bear grew larger and larger, until—

POP!

Out stepped Billy, Milly and Grandpa. They set off for home singing all the way.

You can guess what they were singing: 'Sody, sody, sody saleratus.'

By the time they got home, Ma had been to the store herself and she was mixing flour, butter, milk, a small pinch of salt and, of course, a large pinch of sody saleratus. She made the most meltingly beautiful scones they had ever tasted.

Ma had one. Grandpa had two. Did

Billy and Milly have three? No, I'm afraid they had a lot more than that because they were so delicious. But they wouldn't have tasted half so good if it hadn't been for the

Sody, sody, sody saleratus.

This story is by Pat Thomson.

Sock Eater

Hundred Legs had lots of socks, maybe thousands. Mostly they were long socks, which he pulled up over his knees to keep them warm. He had red socks and green, blue socks and brown, grey, black and Argyle. He had socks with embroidered clocks on the sides. And striped socks, darned socks, old socks and holey socks but very few new socks. And *never ever* enough socks of matching kind and colour.

So, when the invitation came to

Grasshopper's wedding, off he went to buy one hundred brand-new socks, one hundred, red-and-white-striped, long socks, all exactly alike.

'I'll wash them before I wear them,' he fussed, tearing the packages off the socks and tossing them into the washing machine.

Slish-slosh! The machine washed, swirling one hundred socks in froth and bubbles.

Whizz-whizz! It spun.

Swish-swirl! It rinsed.

Whizz-whizz! It spun.

Stretch-peg! Hundred Legs hung the socks on the line to dry.

On the wedding morning he started to pull on his freshly-washed, sun-dried, brand-new, red-and-white-striped, long socks. It took him a long time. All at once he had no more socks!

And two of his feet were still bare!

No more socks! Hundred Legs was astonished.

Hadn't he bought one hundred socks, one for each foot? Yes, he had.

Had he or hadn't he put those one hundred, red-and-white-striped, long socks into the washing machine? Yes, he had.

Hadn't the machine washed them and rinsed them and spun them? Yes it had.

And hadn't he pegged them on the line to dry in the sun? Yes he had. Yes. *Yes!*

But . . . did he count the socks? *No!*

'I'll just have to have a sock hunt,' he said.

Hundred Legs looked in the washing machine. No socks there!

He looked in the garden and under the clothes-line. No socks! He looked in

drawers. He looked in cupboards and on the floors, under cushions and behind the doors. Under chairs and under the telly. In the oven and in the fridge. In the dustbin. Under the piano lid. In cake tins and saucepans, baskets and milk jugs, bottles and tins, and under every mat in the house. No socks! No socks were found. No newly-washed, sun-dried, red-and-white-striped, long socks. He found other things. Under his bed were two lost jumpers, an old apple core and lots of dust. There was plenty of fluff and heaps of dirty socks. In piles, raggy-taggy piles. And socks stuffed into the toes of old shoes.

'I'm still going to Grasshopper's wedding no matter what!' he said, picking up two odd socks, a green and a blue. He put them on. Mmmmm! His feet looked different. Rather smart, he thought. Hmmmm! He admired them in the mirror. At the same time he saw his red–and–white striped, long socks. 'Oh, no! No! No! *No!*' he wailed.

His brand–new socks, the freshly washed, sun–dried, red–and–white–striped, long socks were dirty. Absolutely filthy! He had gone on his sock hunt without his shoes.

Off came the dirty socks. Into the washing machine. *Slosh-swish!* It started to wash and Hundred Legs humped off to make his bed which had four legs.

Slosh-slosh, chugga-chugga-chugga-ugga-ugga-ugg-ugg-clonk-ugg-clonk-onk-clonk! Bang! The washing machine stopped. Something smelt nasty and burnt. Hundred Legs rushed to the laundry. He turned off the machine. He bailed out the water and his socks. He wrung and he twisted and squeezed water from every one. He was too tired to count the socks as he slung them over the line to dry in the sun. And dry they were by wedding time.

One by one he put them on. It took a long time. Then there were no more socks left – again! Again! And Hundred Legs had more than two bare feet, more bare feet than he could count.

'Someone is pinching my socks!' he muttered. 'How can I go to the wedding now?'

He badly wanted to go. And he did. In bare feet.

It was a lovely wedding.

Next morning, not too early, he pulled the washing machine to pieces. He tapped and tinkered, screwed and poked, pried and prodded, then pulled from its innards a long, skinny, slippery, greasy, red-and-whitish thing. Then another and another and another and another! What in the world were they?

Hundred Legs held one high. He

looked at it in every way. He even smelt it. Then he yelled, 'So, you're the dirty-sock eater!' And he gave the washing machine a good, hard thump.

It just stood there, just stood, of course. Later, it did wash Hundred Legs' socks again – and very clean they were – but it never ate another one.

Hundred Legs always carefully put his dirty socks into pillow slips before dropping them into the machine. So he still had one hundred, red-and-white-striped, long socks to wear to weddings and on other important occasions.

This story is by Jean Chapman.

Marika's Favourite Story

Marika loved going to spend the
night with her grannie. She lived in a
flat with a long narrow hall where
Marika could play skittles before supper.

Supper was different from supper at
home. At home Marika had baked
beans on toast, or scrambled egg at the
kitchen table. But at Grannie's she sat in
the dining room on a beautiful old chair
at a beautiful shiny table. She had a mat
of her own with pictures of huntsmen on
it and even a little mat under her glass
of apple juice. Grannie gave her a plate

with ham rolled up and radishes and crisp white rolls speckled with poppyseed. Round the ham she made patterns in strips of sliced red peppers and green peppers. For pudding Marika had a bowl of nuts and raisins and a bunch of grapes or a satsuma from the fruit bowl.

When she got down from supper she always went to the sitting room, straight to Grannie's glass cabinet – a small cupboard full of windows – to stare at all the treasures. There were fans made of ivory and pieces of lace as fine as cobwebs.

There were cups and saucers painted with gold. There was a china shepherdess and a china cow. There was a little silver chair and a box in the shape of a heart with 'I love you' written on it in spidery writing. And last, not least, there was the little wooden cat.

Marika and Grannie would look at every single thing very carefully, always leaving the little wooden cat till last, and then Marika would sit down on the stool by Grannie in her chair and say, 'Now, please, Grannie, tell me again. Tell me my favourite story.'

'Are you sure you want the same story?' asked Grannie.

'I am sure,' said Marika.

'All right,' said Grannie. 'Long ago there was a little girl called Marika . . .'

'And she was your mother, wasn't she, Grannie?'

'Yes. My mother, who lived in a beautiful city . . .'

'Where all the churches had domes like onions instead of towers,' said Marika, 'but onions made of gold . . .'

'Yes,' said Grannie. 'And Marika lived with her mother and father near the river by the bridge . . .'

'And that Marika's mother was called Marika, too, like you, Grannie, and me. We are a long chain of Marikas . . .'

'Yes,' said Grannie. 'Who's telling this story to who?'

'I was just starting you off,' said Marika.

'One day Marika fell ill. She had a very bad cough and it just would not go away, so her mother and father took her to the mountains to stay with . . .'

'Another Marika!' said Marika happily. 'Your mother's mother's mother!'

'Yes,' said Grannie. 'Old Marika. She lived on a farm far away from the town . . . all by herself except for her cow and her horse and cart, and her chickens and her pig and her apple trees and her grapevine.

'Little Marika soon felt much better up there in the fresh air. Old Marika taught her how to make butter and cheese, and to pick apples and grapes and let her feed the chickens and collect the warm eggs every morning from the nests.

'One day she said, "Tomorrow is market day and you must come to town with me."

'Next morning, old Marika harnessed her horse to her cart and little Marika helped her put all the butter, eggs, cheese and fruit into the cart.

'And off they went to market. The town was very small. There was a square in the middle with a fountain and a church and a few shops.

'Little Marika was very excited. She had not been to town for a long time.

'"Oh," she cried. "Can I go shopping now, Grannie?"

'"No," said old Marika. "First you must help me unload the cart and put out the things to sell."

'"Oh," said little Marika sadly.

'"Then you can go round and look at all the things there are to buy, but just look, mind, not buy."

'"Oh," said little Marika.

'"And then, at the end of the day, before we go home, you can choose something for yourself and I will give it to you as a present so you will always remember staying with me."

'"Oh!" said little Marika happily.

'All the farmers like old Marika had set up stalls to sell their vegetables and fruit and flowers.

'Little Marika worked hard to help her grandmother. Then old Marika said, "That's enough now. Off you go to look and choose!"

'Little Marika ran off gaily. She walked round the square looking in each shop window one by one.

'She looked at the baker's and at the

sweet shop because she was hungry.

'"No," she said. "I won't buy a bun or a lollipop because if I eat them I will not have them to remind me of staying with old Marika. I will choose a toy, or a book or a pretty picture."

'But she could not find a toyshop or a bookshop or any pretty pictures. The town was very small, not like the big city where she lived with her parents which had shops of every kind you can imagine.

'Here there was just a grocer's shop and a shop full of string and buckets and brooms and a shop full of dull warm clothes for grown-ups and, at the last corner, a shoemaker's.

'She saw the shoemaker sitting near his window to catch the light.

'"I don't want a pair of shoes," she sighed, "or a bucket, or a bag of flour, or a bun or a lollipop." And she began

to turn away sadly. But what was the
shoemaker doing? He wasn't making
shoes. He wasn't mending shoes. He
was carving something out of a piece of
wood and, by the shape of his mouth,
she could see he was whistling. He
looked up and smiled at her and held up
a little wooden cat.

'"Oh!" cried little Marika. "That's it.
That's what I want!"

'And she flew back to old Marika
and tugged at her hand.

'"I've found it!" she said. "I've found
the very thing I want to remember you
by."

'"Just a minute, just a minute!"
laughed old Marika. "Can't you wait
even a minute?"

'"No!" said little Marika and she
dragged her grandmother to the
shoemaker's. And when she saw the
little wooden cat she smiled and said,

"Now that's nice," and took out a big coin from her purse and paid the shoemaker and gave Marika the little wooden cat and a big fat kiss.'

'And then they went home,' put in Marika.

'Yes,' said Grannie.

'And little Marika's mother and father soon came and fetched her and she went back with them to the big city. With the little wooden cat.' She sighed happily. 'I love that story,' she said.

'Ahh,' said her grannie. 'But it's not quite the end.'

'Is there a bit I don't know?' asked Marika.

'Oh yes,' said Grannie. 'You never asked so I never told you: how does the little wooden cat come to be in my glass cabinet?'

'No!' said Marika. 'I never did ask, did I? How did you get it?'

'Well,' said Grannie. 'When that little Marika was about ten there was a war in her country and she had to run away with her mother and father and come to this country to be safe.'

'Oh,' said Marika. 'How terrible.'

'Yes,' said her grannie. 'They had to leave in a hurry, but before they left, little Marika's mother said to her "You can bring one small thing which you couldn't bear to leave behind." And, of course, she chose . . .'

'The little wooden cat,' said Marika.

'Yes,' said Grannie. 'And when I was about your age she gave it to me.'

'And did she tell you the story too?'

'Of course,' said Grannie.

'And was it your favourite story?'

'Of course,' said Grannie. 'But even that's not quite the end.'

And she got up and went to the glass cabinet and opened the door.

'Here you are, Marika. Now you take the little wooden cat home with you and perhaps one day you can tell the story to another little Marika . . .'

'Who will tell it to another little Marika,' said Marika sleepily, 'and she will tell it to another little Marika and on and on and on . . . so it will always be Marika's favourite story.'

This story is by Jenny Koralek.

Haddock

There was once a haddock who fell in love with a mermaid. He gave her fishy gifts and followed her everywhere, from the depths to the shallows, but there were places where even a haddock could not go. For the mermaid liked to sit upon a rock and make eyes at passing fishermen. The haddock could only bob alongside and blow devoted bubbles.

'O come with me to the bottom of the sea,' the haddock sang.

'Stick to your own kind,' the mermaid said, while the scales on her tail clinked scornfully.

'But you are my kind,' the haddock said, and sank below the surface.

The mermaid hoped to marry a mortal man and live upon land, but from where the haddock was looking, she was all fish.

Every day the mermaid sang to the fishermen, but the fishermen put limpets in their ears and rowed rapidly away from the mermaid. Their mothers had warned them about girls like her.

There was one fisherman whose mother had run off to live in a lighthouse, so he had no-one to give him good advice. His name was Stanley. When he heard the mermaid singing he steered close to the rock.

'Nice weather we're having,' Stanley said. The mermaid smiled and all the scales on her tail chimed harmoniously.

After that, Stanley came back every day.

'Take me home with you, Stanley, and make me your fishwife,' the mermaid said, twirling her tail.

'There are ten steps up to the front door,' said Stanley, and he looked at the tail.

'I'll sing to you all day, Stanley,' the mermaid said, and she began to sing there and then, upon the rock. Stanley wondered what the neighbours would say.

Night came and the mermaid dived back into the water.

The haddock was waiting. 'I love you,' the haddock said.

'My heart belongs to Stanley,' the mermaid said. 'Stanley eats people like you for breakfast.'

'I know,' said the haddock, sadly. 'Fishwives cook us with rice and call it kedgeree.'

When daylight came the mermaid sat

upon the rock and combed her hair while the haddock hung about humbly where her tail fins touched the foam.

'Go away,' the mermaid cried, when she saw Stanley's boat put out from the shore. But the haddock would not go.

'Kedgeree, kedgeree,' the mermaid hissed. It was the worst thing that she could think of.

Then Stanley's boat went by and in the stern sat a bold handsome woman. It was Moll the fishwife in her best serge skirt, with a bustle. Moll also fancied Stanley. Stanley looked at the mermaid, and he looked at Moll. Moll looked at the mermaid.

'I wouldn't have a tail for all the world,' said Moll. 'Not if you *paid* me, I wouldn't have a tail.'

The mermaid looked at Moll's serge skirt with the bustle.

Next morning when she sat upon the

rock she was fetchingly decked out in an old fishing net. Round the back, under the net, was a lobster pot. Stanley brought his boat very close to the rock and seemed impressed.

The haddock saw the fishing net and when the mermaid came down that evening he was waiting for her with a few strands of bladderwrack wrapped round his fins.

'I love you,' said the haddock.

'How ridiculous you look,' the mermaid said, and punctured several of the bladders with a fishbone.

The haddock went away and wept bitter tears, but as they were fifteen fathoms down, nobody noticed.

Next day the mermaid sat upon her rock, fanning herself with a flounder, and Stanley's boat came nigh. Stanley stood up in the stern just as the haddock broke the surface.

'O come with me to the bottom of the sea,' the haddock cried.

'Come instead to my bonny boat and we'll be wed,' said Stanley.

'Oh, Stanley, yes!' the mermaid gasped.

Stanley steered his boat dangerously near to the rock and the mermaid slithered aboard.

'Don't forget your fishing net,' said Stanley. He was still worried about the neighbours.

'Come back, come back,' the haddock begged, but at that moment his fins stuck fast in the mermaid's skirt and he was dragged on board behind her.

'I see you've brought our wedding breakfast with you,' Stanley said, and he whipped out his fish knife. The haddock raised his fin in a final salute.

'Farewell, beloved. Remember, when you eat your kedgeree, that you are

eating me,' he whispered, and prepared
to breathe his last. At those words the
mermaid understood that she could
never be a fishwife. She rose up on her
tail fins and turned on Stanley.

'You brute!' she cried, and hit him in
the eye with her flounder.

Then she seized the haddock in her
arms and leaped over the side.

Down below, the mermaid and the
haddock gazed deep into each other's
eyes.

'What a blind fool I've been,' the
mermaid said. 'Can you ever forgive
me?'

'I love you,' said the haddock.

'Huh! Women!' said Stanley, and
turned his boat for the shore, where
Moll was waiting.

'Huh! Fish!' said Moll. 'I warned you
about girls like her.'

Stanley married Moll and after ten

years they had seven children.

But the mermaid and the haddock had thousands – all at once.

This story is by Jan Mark.

The Town Mouse and
the Country Mouse

Beneath the hedge where the roots were tangled, there was a little door. In the door was a tiny letter box and behind the door stood Country Mouse holding something in her hand.

'A letter,' squeaked Country Mouse. 'A letter for me!' She hardly ever had a letter.

'It's a letter from my cousin Town Mouse. Fancy that! He has written me a letter. What can he want?' She began to read.

'My Dear Cousin,

I am tired of town life. It has become so hot and noisy, so disagreeable. I thought of your charming cottage, of the delicious flowers, the cool green of the grass and I decided to visit you. Pray don't give yourself any trouble, my dear. A simple bed and plain food is all I need. Expect me tomorrow.

Your affectionate relation,
Town Mouse.

'Tomorrow!' gasped Country Mouse. 'I shall never be ready!'

She took her brush and swept her little house from top to bottom. She made a bed of fresh hay in her visitor's room and polished her best table with beeswax.

Then she took her basket and bustled out to collect seeds and berries, nuts and fruits from the fields and hedges.

It was late when she went to bed but everything was ready for her guest.

When her cousin strolled up her path the next day, Country Mouse was dazzled by his smartness.

His coat was an elegant grey. His fur was smoothly parted. Over his arm, he carried a rolled umbrella and his fashionably thin tail. He twirled his whiskers most impressively.

'My dear Cousin,' he said, 'what a delightful little cottage you have. A tiny treasure. How beautifully arranged.'

'Please sit down, Cousin, and be comfortable,' replied Country Mouse. 'You must be hungry,' and she began to serve the food and offer acorn cups of water from the spring.

'Charming,' said Town Mouse. 'Seeds? How unusual. Still, they do say a change is as good as a rest. I've been overdoing it lately. I'm afraid I've been rattling around town, enjoying myself.'

'Then you must rest,' insisted Country Mouse, kindly. 'Enjoy the peace of the country and go early to bed.'

'Early to bed!' laughed the Town Mouse. 'Why, of course, in the country, one goes early to bed. I must try it.'

The next morning, however, Town Mouse came down to breakfast full of complaints.

'Such a night!' he groaned. 'I never slept for a moment. In town, we have feather beds. Hay is so prickly.'

Country Mouse was worried for her guest. 'I'm so sorry,' she said. 'We always have hay beds in the country. I love the smell of freshly cut hay.'

'I love the smell of fresh bacon,' answered Town Mouse. 'Have you a little bacon? A sliver of cheese? One cannot live on berries and such things, you know.'

Country Mouse knew that she did but she was too polite to say so. She decided that she would take her cousin on a country walk. He would see such beautiful flowers, such magnificent trees and smell the wonderful scents of the wood. Then, surely, he would cheer up. But he did not.

'Your country paths are so uneven,' he grumbled as he tottered along on his delicate town feet. He grumbled and grumbled. 'This grass is making me sneeze. How dusty the path is. How much further must we walk?'

'Sssh!' warned Country Mouse, sniffing the air. 'I think Weasel is in the wood.'

Town Mouse very nearly fainted, and as they returned and the first owls began to hoot, he scampered back to the cottage as fast as he could.

'My dear Country Mouse,' he said as

he lay in her best armchair that evening, his feet on a mossy cushion, 'how can you bear to live in the country? I insist that you pay me a visit. You will see how we live in town. You will love the soft beds, the different things to eat, the lights and entertainment. Come back with me tomorrow.'

Country Mouse listened to him as he described the town. What a great, glowing place it seemed. Everything was plentiful and comfortable and a mouse need never work. She would go on this adventure and see a town at last.

Country Mouse knew they were reaching the town when she saw the lights. She had never seen so many in her life. Then she saw the buildings: huge, towering houses. She followed close behind Town Mouse, afraid she would lose him.

Then Town Mouse pointed to a tall house with a front door almost as big as a barn door.

'My house,' he said, proudly. 'This way.' But he did not go to the front door. He led Country Mouse to some stone steps and they ran down them, along the wall and into a little, dark hole.

Country Mouse found herself in a long, dark passage. Other passages led off to right and left and strange smells came from all directions.

'First, a little supper after our journey,' declared Town Mouse. 'This way, through this hole.'

Country Mouse was dazzled by the brightness of the vast room. There was a huge table in the middle of it and she ran with her bold cousin across the stone-flagged floor and up the table leg.

It was all true! She had never seen

such a feast! There was meat, bread, cakes and things Country Mouse had never seen before. She darted from plate to plate, nibbling here and nibbling there until a dreadful shrieking noise made her heart almost stop.

'Run! It's Cook,' shouted Town Mouse.

Country Mouse did not know what 'Cook' was but she ran blindly down the table leg, across the floor to where a big door stood open. She rushed through and crouched, panting, behind an enormous armchair.

What should she do? Where should she go?

She peeped around the chair and saw a blazing fire dancing in the hearth. In front of the fire lay a dark shape. As she peered at it, an ear wiggled. A tail twitched. An eye opened. A fierce, green eye. The cat!

Country Mouse ran. She could not find the door. She ran round and round the room, not knowing what she was doing. The cat was standing up. He was watching, then crouching. He was ready to spring.

'This way,' hissed a voice. She saw Town Mouse, peering out of a little hole in the skirting board. He pulled her in and the cat landed on the floorboards and nothing else.

'What a joke,' chortled the Town Mouse. 'I just love annoying that cat!'

But Country Mouse could hardly breathe, she was so frightened.

She spent a restless night. Although the bed was soft, she thought she heard the scritch, scritch of the cat's claws at the mouse hole door. Town life was too adventurous for her.

The next morning, she spoke politely but firmly to Town Mouse. 'My dear

Cousin,' she said, 'you are very kind to invite me to stay but I have decided that town life suits you and country life suits me. I shall go back to my little house under the hedge and live a country life.'

'Perhaps that is wise,' agreed her Cousin, 'but do write to me. The country is so charming. It will be a delight to read about it.'

'You must write back,' said Country Mouse. 'Although I could not live in the town myself, it will be so exciting to hear of your adventures.'

Country Mouse returned to her home and her cousin continued to live in town. Sometimes, Country Mouse sent him a flower and he wore it in his buttonhole, praising the delights of the country. By return, he would send a crumb of the best cheese and Country Mouse would invite all her friends to a feast when they would sigh and declare how wonderful town life must be.

And so they were both happy and satisfied.

This story is a re-telling by Pat Thomson of a traditional story.

A Shaggy Dog Story

Timmy sat on the back step and watched Ginger. The cat washed first one paw and then the other. Timmy sighed. He loved Ginger very much but he did so want a dog.

'You see, a dog will run after a ball or fetch a stick,' he told Ginger. 'Cats don't do that.'

He wondered if Ginger would fetch something. After all, he was a very special cat. Timmy picked up a twig and threw it down the garden. Ginger ignored it and began to wash the tip of his tail.

'Just as I thought!' Timmy said, sadly. 'Dogs are different. You can take dogs for walks, and give them baths and teach them tricks.'

Ginger yawned to show that he thought dogs were boring.

'It doesn't have to be a big dog,' Timmy went on. 'A little dog would do.'

He went into the kitchen where Dad was peeling some potatoes.

'Are you sure I can't have a dog?' Timmy asked.

Dad smiled. 'No, no, a thousand times no!' he said. 'I've told you before, dogs cost money. They have to be fed and if they get ill you have to call in the vet. We can't afford vet's bills. But cheer up, Timmy. You've got Ginger, remember.'

'But he's not a dog,' Timmy muttered, so Dad couldn't hear. Then he sighed noisily and went into the front garden.

He stood on the bottom rung of the gate and looked up and down the road. A man walked past with a poodle on a lead and Timmy sighed again.

Suddenly, he saw an enormous dog hurrying along the pavement. It was black and white and very shaggy and Timmy thought it looked rather worried.

He called, 'Here, boy!' and the big shaggy dog rushed up to him. He wagged his tail and barked and jumped up and down at the gate.

'Are you pleased to see me, then?' asked Timmy, smiling broadly. He looked over the gate, expecting to see the dog's owner, but the road was empty. He opened the gate and the dog bounced in and started to run round the garden. He was so big he made the garden look very small.

Timmy looked for his collar but he was not wearing one. Timmy's eyes grew wider and wider. This dog was a stray.

'Come on, boy!' he shouted and ran to the back of the house. The dog ran after him and they both burst into the kitchen.

'Steady on!' cried Dad.

Mum was pulling on her wellies.

'Whatever's that?' she asked. 'It looks like a walking hearth rug!'

'It's a dog,' said Timmy. 'A stray dog! And it's hungry. It wants a biscuit.'

'How can you tell!' asked Mum. 'It's so shaggy, you can't see its eyes.'

Carefully, Timmy tidied away some of the shaggy hair and they all looked at the dog's brown eyes.

'His name's Shaggy,' said Timmy.

'Oh, has he got a name on his collar?' said Dad. 'Maybe his address is on it, too.'

Timmy explained that he did not have a collar.

'Then how do you know his name?' asked Dad.

'I don't,' said Timmy, 'but it seems a good name for him.'

Dad looked at Mum.

'Look, Timmy,' said Mum. 'We can't keep him, so you mustn't get any ideas in your head. Someone must be looking for him right now. It would be stealing to keep a dog that doesn't belong to us.'

'But we could keep him just for tonight?' Timmy suggested, hopefully. 'In the morning, we could look for his owners.'

He was thinking that he could make a collar and lead out of string and take Shaggy for a walk. They could go to the park. Shaggy could run after a ball, or fetch sticks!

'We really ought to notify the police,'

said Dad. 'They look after lost dogs.'

Timmy was horrified. 'We can't do that!' he cried. 'They might put him in the dog pound. We might never see him again.'

There was a long silence.

Mum, Dad and Timmy all stared at Shaggy and he stared back, wagging his tail.

'You're right,' said Mum, at last. 'We can't do that.'

At that moment there was a rattle at the letterbox. It was Timmy's job to bring in the letters, so he hurried up to the front door. Through the glass he could see the outline of the postman, so he opened the door. The postman handed him a small package.

'This won't go through the letterbox,' he said.

'Thank you,' said Timmy.

As the postman went out through the

gate, a girl came in. She was about the
same age as Timmy and she looked
very upset. She had ginger hair and
grey eyes, and she looked as though she
had been crying.

Timmy went down to the gate.

'My name's Sarah,' she said. 'I'm
looking for my dog—'

Before she could say any more,
Timmy said quickly, 'We have a dog
called Shaggy.'

As soon as he said it, he felt terrible.
He had told a lie.

'My dog's called Bruno,' she said.
'We've just moved into Number
Seventy-one and while the men were
carrying in the furniture, Bruno ran
away.'

Still Timmy said nothing. He had
wanted a dog for so long and now he
had found Shaggy. He couldn't bear to
let him go.

'He's a big dog,' Sarah went on. 'Black and white.'

Timmy heard himself say, 'Have you looked in the park?'

'I've looked everywhere,' she told him. 'I've been round and round the streets and Mum has phoned the police.'

'They might find him,' said Timmy.

His voice sounded different and he felt sort of shaky. He knew he ought to tell her the truth, but if he did, she would take Shaggy away.

'I'll just have to keep looking,' said Sarah. 'I'm so afraid he'll go into the road and get run over.'

'I hope you find him,' Timmy said.

He ran back into the house and shut the door. He felt very confused. It was all the postman's fault, he told himself. If I hadn't had to open the door to the postman, I would never have met Sarah.

Then I wouldn't know that she was Shaggy's owner.

She had seemed a nice girl and Timmy did not want to feel sorry for her.

He went back into the kitchen. Mum had broken up some bread and was mixing it with a tin of meat soup.

'If Shaggy's hungry, he'll eat this,' she said.

Timmy nodded. He gave the package to Dad.

'Oh good!' said Dad. 'It's the seeds I ordered. I'll sow them in the garden tomorrow.'

Timmy looked at him. Whatever would Dad say if he told him about the lie?

Mum handed the plate of food to Timmy. 'You give it to him,' she said.

Without a word, Timmy put the food on the floor and Shaggy sniffed at it. Then he sat down and began to scratch his ear.

'You must eat,' Timmy told him.

'He's pining,' said Mum.

'He's not pining,' said Timmy. 'He'll eat it. I know he will.'

He knelt down on the floor beside the bowl of food and pretended to eat it, with loud gobbling noises.

'Yum, yum!' he said. 'What a delicious dinner. Meat and bread. How scrumptious. You'd better hurry up, Shaggy, or I shall eat it all!'

Shaggy watched him sadly. They tried everything they could think of but nothing they did would persuade him to eat.

Dad said, 'I know what we'll do. I'll write a notice and we'll pin it to the gatepost. We'll say we've found a dog and then if the owner is looking for—'

'If I had some string, I could take Shaggy for a walk,' Timmy said.

At the word 'walk', Shaggy pricked up his ears.

Dad found an old leather belt and made a comfortable collar for Shaggy to wear. He made a lead out of a length of cord.

'There!' he said, proudly.

Timmy tried to smile but his lips felt stiff. He wanted to get out of the house so that he could think.

He and Shaggy set off along the road towards the park but half-way there Timmy had a dreadful thought: Sarah might be there, looking for Bruno.

'I'm sorry, Shaggy,' he said. 'We'll walk around the block instead.'

But suppose Sarah was still walking up and down the street?

'Blow it!' cried Timmy. 'Blow, blast and botheration!'

He went home again and Mum and Dad looked up in surprise.

'I've changed my mind,' Timmy told them. 'Shaggy might run away in the park. I think we'll play in the garden instead.'

Mum and Dad looked at each other.

'Is anything wrong, Timmy?' Mum asked.

'No,' said Timmy and he hurried out into the garden.

Ginger was playing on the grass with a dry leaf but as soon as he saw Shaggy, he ran up the pear tree. Shaggy lolloped after him, barking with excitement.

'Stop that!' said Timmy. 'Leave Ginger alone.' He found an old tennis ball and threw it down the garden. 'Fetch it, boy!'

Shaggy rushed after the ball and carried it back in his mouth. For the next half an hour they had a marvellous game and Timmy began to feel happier.

When they went back into the kitchen they were both panting.

'Look,' said Dad and he held up a notice. It was written in red ink.

FOUND:

LARGE BLACK-AND-WHITE DOG

'What do you think?' asked Dad.

'It's fine,' said Timmy.

Dad went into the front garden and pinned the notice to the gate.

When Timmy went to bed that night, Shaggy went to sleep on a cushion in the kitchen.

Timmy tried to get to sleep but he was too worried. He thought that Sarah might see the notice in the morning and guess the truth. He would tell Mum and Dad and they would know about his lie.

He lay awake, staring up into the

darkness. He thought it was the worst night in his whole life.

Suddenly, he heard a strange wailing noise and sat up in bed. The noise went on and on. Timmy had never heard anything like it before but at last he realized what it was.

Shaggy was howling.

Timmy jumped out of bed and ran downstairs.

Shaggy was standing by the back door, looking very sad.

Mum arrived in her dressing-gown.

'I hope he's not going to howl all night,' she said. 'We shan't get any sleep.'

'Perhaps he's lonely,' said Timmy.

'He's homesick,' said Mum. 'He misses his owners. How would you feel if you were lost and had to sleep in a house full of strangers?'

'Perhaps he would sleep better in my room,' suggested Timmy. He thought

Mum would say 'No' but she said, 'Yes.'

'Anything for a bit of peace and quiet,' she added.

Timmy took Shaggy upstairs and let him sleep on the bottom of his bed. Shaggy snored quietly but Timmy stayed awake for a long time, thinking.

It rained in the night and Dad's notice was ruined. The rain had washed all the red letters away.

'Oh dear,' said Mum. 'We'll have to make another one. I'll do it after I've taken you to school.'

Timmy finished his breakfast.

'Will Shaggy be here when I get back?' he asked.

'I don't know,' said Mum.

Timmy said goodbye to Shaggy and gave him a big hug.

He went to school and met some of his friends in the playground but he did not feel like playing. He stood by himself near the railings and was so busy with his thoughts that he didn't see Sarah arrive.

'Hello,' she said.

Timmy stared at her. 'Do you go to this school, then?' he asked.

'I do now,' she said. 'This is my first day. What's it like?'

'It's fine,' said Timmy.

She looked very nervous and Timmy felt sorry for her. She had just moved house and she had lost her dog. Now she was starting at a new school. He wanted to say, 'Have you found Bruno?' but the words seem to stick in his throat.

Instead he said, 'I found your dog. I found Bruno.'

Sarah's expression changed at once. 'You've found him? How? Where? Oh, thank goodness he's safe!'

She was smiling and Timmy smiled with her.

He felt a rush of courage. 'I found him yesterday,' he confessed. 'Before I met you.'

'Oh!' she said. She gave him a funny look. Timmy thought she would be angry but she just looked at him without saying anything.

He felt very hot and uncomfortable.

'I'm sorry,' he said. 'I should have told you yesterday.'

Sarah said, 'Never mind. You've told me now.'

'I took great care of Shaggy – I mean Bruno,' he told her. 'Mum let him sleep on my bed because he was howling.'

She laughed. 'Did he snore? He does, sometimes.'

'Yes, he did.' Timmy sighed. 'I wanted to pretend he was mine, just for a little while.'

Sarah looked at him thoughtfully. 'We could share him, if you like.'

Timmy gasped. 'Share him? Do you really mean it?'

She nodded. 'We could take him to the park together and we could take turns to brush him. Having a dog is hard work.'

'If you were ill, I could look after him for you,' Timmy said, eagerly. 'And I could buy him a tin of dog food once a week out of my pocket money.'

'You could take him for a walk on Thursdays when I go to tap-dancing lessons,' said Sarah.

Timmy's mind was racing. 'I could bring him to meet you from the tap-dancing class.'

'It would be fun,' she said.

They smiled at each other.

'We'll shake on it,' Sarah said. 'Like this.'

She held out her right hand and they shook hands. Then she held out her left hand and they shook again. Just then the bell rang and all the children stood still.

'What's happening?' asked Sarah.

'Another bell rings,' he told her, 'and we all find a partner and line up.'

'Oh dear. I don't know anyone,' she said.

'You know me!' said Timmy and they both laughed. They stood together in the line and Timmy felt very happy.

He was not going to lose Shaggy, after all. He was going to share him with Sarah and that was even better than having him all to himself. He should have realized that a dog like Shaggy was too much work for one person.

'I must remember to call him Bruno!' he said and went into school grinning all over his face.

This story is by Pamela Oldfield.

A BUS FULL OF STORIES
FOR FOUR YEAR OLDS
Collected by Pat Thomson

Catch this bus and meet . . . a cat
with a special talent, a naughty cow,
a little boy who runs away from
home, a bear who likes hugging
people and many other jolly and
exciting characters and animals. You
won't want to stop listening as the bus
bounces along from story to story!

**'A marvellous anthology of short
stories by some top children's
writers . . . perfect for
reading aloud'**
Daily Telegraph

ISBN 0 552 52816 1

CORGI BOOKS

A BUCKETFUL OF STORIES
FOR SIX YEAR OLDS
Collected by Pat Thomson

Dip into this bucketful of stories and
you will find . . . a ghost who lives in
a cupboard, a dog that saves a ship, a
king who can turn things into gold, a
dwarf who becomes a cat, and many
other strange and exciting creatures.
You won't want to stop reading until
you get right to the bottom of the
bucket!

**'Well suited to the stated age
group . . . the mixture seems
guaranteed to please'**
The Times Educational Supplement

ISBN 0 552 52757 2

Now available from all good book stores

CORGI BOOKS

A BAND OF JOINING-IN STORIES

Collected by Pat Thomson
Illustrated by Steve Cox

Here's a great, action-packed collection of stories – one where children join in!

There are rhythms to clap along with, actions to copy, animal noises and repeated choruses as young listeners join in with a lion hunt, discover the Rajah's big secret, meet the fattest of fat cats – and even outwit a fearsome troll!

ISBN 0 552 52815 3

Now available in all good book stores

CORGI BOOKS

A BARREL OF STORIES FOR SEVEN YEAR OLDS
Collected by Pat Thomson

Roll out the barrel and discover naughty Angela and her sticky school trick; Frankel, the farmer who outwits the Czar; Ignatius Binz, a boy with a truly magnificent nose; a Hallowe'en trick that goes wrong; and a whole host of other wonderful characters and stories. You won't want to stop reading until you get right to the bottom of the barrel!

'Lively and rich collections of stories for all ages'
Books for Keeps

ISBN 0 552 52817 X

CORGI BOOKS

A BED FULL OF NIGHT-TIME STORIES

Collected by Pat Thomson
Illustrated by Anthony Lewis

Snuggle up in bed with these
wonderful stories.

By the light of the full moon, travel on
a flying quilt, dance with twelve
princesses, or learn how to make a
ghost disappear. Here are tales
wrapped in the magic and mystery of
night-time from such well-loved
authors as Joan Aiken, Helen
Cresswell, Dick King-Smith and
Philippa Pearce.

**'Pat Thomson's story collections
are always fresh, rich and
entertaining'**
Books For Keeps

ISBN 0 552 52961 3

CORGI BOOKS